THE YOUNG JEDI

Written by Emeli Juhlin

Based on the episode "The Young Jedi,"
by Michael Olson

PRESS

LOS ANGELES • NEW YORK

This is Master Yoda.
He is visiting younglings.
Younglings are children
training to become Jedi Knights.
Jedi Knights protect the galaxy.
The younglings are being sent
to faraway temples to continue
to learn, explore, and help others.

Kai Brightstar, Lys Solay, and Nubs miss Yoda's visit.
They are trying to break their training record.

Kai thinks he can do it alone.
He tells his friends
he does not need help.
But he cannot stop the droids!

Lys tells Kai he does not need to do it alone.

When they work together,
they break their record!

Master Zia is their teacher.

She calls the younglings.

The shuttles are leaving!

Kai, Lys, and Nubs must hurry.

This is the *Crimson Firehawk*.
It is the last shuttle to Tenoo.

Nash Durango and RJ-83
pilot the *Crimson Firehawk*.
They will take the younglings
to their new temple on Tenoo.

Nash's moms own a shuttle company. They transport anything and anyone all over the galaxy!

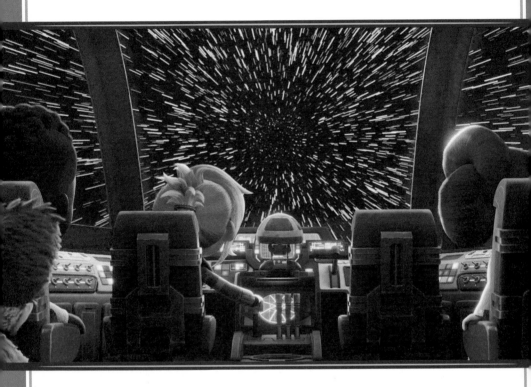

The crew put on their seat belts.
Nash loves to fly fast.

On their way to Tenoo,
the younglings look around.
Nash has snacks!
Nubs is hungry.
He loves food.

Lys finds a creature
she has never seen before.
Nash is taking it to a new home.
Lys loves creatures.

Kai finds a fun game.
He does not have a lot of time
for games at the temple.
He is too busy training.

Nash gets a call from Hap.

He needs help on Tenoo!

Pirates are stealing from him.

Taborr is a pirate.

He loves to steal things.

He is taking things from Hap.

When the Jedi arrive,
Kai tells Taborr to give back
what he stole.

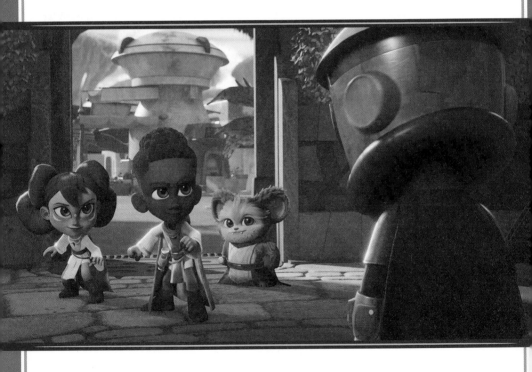

Taborr does not listen.
He does not want to give back
what he stole.

Kai must stop Taborr!
Kai uses his lightsaber.

A lightsaber is a laser sword. Jedi use it only for defense, never to attack.

Lys and Nubs try to stop
Pord and EB-3.
Pord and EB-3 are also pirates.

Taborr cannot stop Kai.
He breaks branches
to distract Kai.

At first, Kai tries to
stop the branches alone.
But he cannot stop the branches!

Kai thinks of the training room.

He knows he needs help.

Lys and Nubs help Kai.

The younglings stop the branches using the Force.
The Force is an energy field that connects all living things.

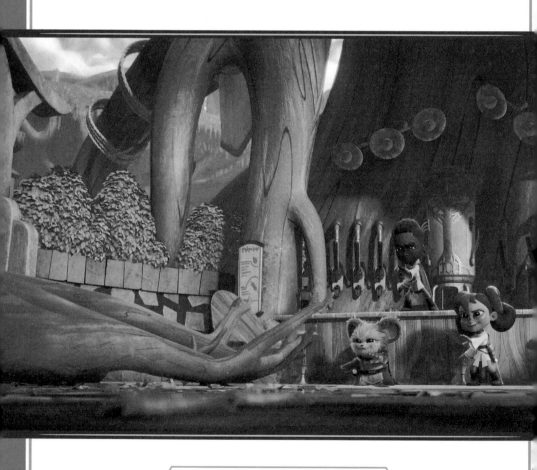

The younglings chase after Taborr.
They have to stop the pirates
before they escape!

The people of Tenoo help
the younglings stop Taborr.

The pirates return
what they stole.

The younglings arrive at the temple.
Master Zia heard what happened.
She is proud that they helped others
and worked together.

Master Zia takes them
on a tour of the Jedi temple.
It is their new home.

The younglings cannot wait
for the next adventure.
They will be great
Jedi Knights someday!